WHEN I GROW UP
I'LL BE AN ENGINEER

BY CONNIE COLWELL MILLER
ILLUSTRATED BY SILVIA BARONCELLI

AMICUS ILLUSTRATED • AMICUS INK

For Anson–C.C.M.

Amicus Illustrated and Amicus Ink are imprints of Amicus
P.O. Box 227, Mankato, MN 56002
www.amicuspublishing.us

LIBRARY OF CONGRESS CATALOGING-IN-PUBLICATION DATA
Names: Miller, Connie Colwell, 1976- author. | Baroncelli, Silvia, illustrator.
Title: I'll be an engineer / by Connie Colwell Miller ; illustrated by Silvia Baroncelli.
Other titles: I will be an engineer | I'll be an engineer when I grow up
Description: Mankato, MN : Amicus/Amicus Ink, [2019] | Series: When I grow up...
Identifiers: LCCN 2017056342 (print) | LCCN 2018002075 (ebook) | ISBN 9781681514833 (pdf) | ISBN 9781681514017 (library binding) | ISBN 9781681523217 (pbk.)
Subjects: LCSH: Civil engineering—Vocational guidance—Juvenile literature.
Classification: LCC TA157 (ebook) | LCC TA157 .M494 2019 (print) | DDC 624 .023—dc23
LC record available at https://lccn.loc.gov/2017056342

EDITOR: Rebecca Glaser
DESIGNER: Kathleen Petelinsek

ABOUT THE AUTHOR

Connie Colwell Miller is a writer, reader, and teacher who lives in Mankato, Minnesota. When she was little she always knew she would work with two things: kids and books. Today, her dream has come true. She has written over 100 books for kids, and she lives with four wonderful, creative children of her own.

ABOUT THE ILLUSTRATOR

Silvia Baroncelli has loved to draw since she was a child. She collaborates regularly with publishers in drawing and graphic design from her home in Prato, Italy. Her best collaborators are her four nephews, daughter Ginevra, and organized husband Tommaso. Find out more about her on the web at silviabaroncelli.it

In the basement, Dad and I build a whole city out of blocks. Our city has roads, tunnels, and even an airport. Sometimes while we're building, I pretend . . .

I am Sunny, a real-life civil engineer. I design and build structures people use every day. I work for the city of Springville. My team and I are going to build a bridge to help people cross this river by car and by foot.

Engineering isn't just building things. First, there is planning! My team and I survey the land where the bridge will be built. We measure the land. We figure out where all the parts of a bridge could go.

Once we know where the bridge will fit, we draw up the plans. I help the architect create a bridge that is sturdy and strong. We design a bridge that will safely hold the weight of the traffic.

That's not all. Springville is a windy city. I use my math and science skills to create a bridge design that can withstand high winds. We also want it to be beautiful. The architect creates a design that fits with the surrounding city.

Next, my team and I choose what materials to use. We figure out how much we need and how much it will cost. Then we order the materials. We need concrete and steel for our bridge.

Finally, we are ready to start building! We need a lot of workers. A contractor hires a crew of construction workers. We give the bridge designs to the contractor. The crew starts on the foundation. I make sure they follow the plans.

It takes months to build a bridge! We have to build the support piers and the flat decks. Workers build from each side. Now the bridge goes across the river.

When the bridge is built, we are still not done. I run tests to make sure the bridge is safe and ready for traffic. I need to keep the people of Springville safe.

Once I'm sure the bridge is well built and safe, it's ready. People drive on it, and people can bike or walk across it, too. I enjoy watching people use something that I helped build!

When I grow up, I'll be a great engineer. But right now, my contractor (I mean, my dad!) and I are having enough fun just pretending.

WORDS AN ENGINEER SHOULD KNOW

architect—A person who designs how structures look.

civil engineer—A person who designs and helps build structures for cities, choosing the right materials and building methods to make safe structures.

contractor—A person who agrees to provide workers and materials to get a job done.

deck—The flat part of the bridge over which cars, people, or trains pass.

foundation—The support structure upon which the rest of the structure rests.

pier—A vertical support column of a bridge.

survey—To precisely measure an area of land in order to make a map or a plan for building.

PRACTICE ENGINEERING BUILD A STRUCTURE

Engineers need to know how to build sturdy structures. Practice by building with toothpicks. Does your structure stand up by itself?

WHAT YOU NEED

Box of toothpicks
Bag of gumdrops or marshmallows

WHAT YOU DO

1. Insert each end of a toothpick into a gumdrop or marshmallow.
2. Now insert a new toothpick into the opposite side of the same gumdrop or marshmallow.
3. Continue to connect toothpicks together using the gumdrops or marshmallows.
4. Experiment with different shapes like cubes and pyramids.
5. Challenge yourself to make a structure that can stand on its own.

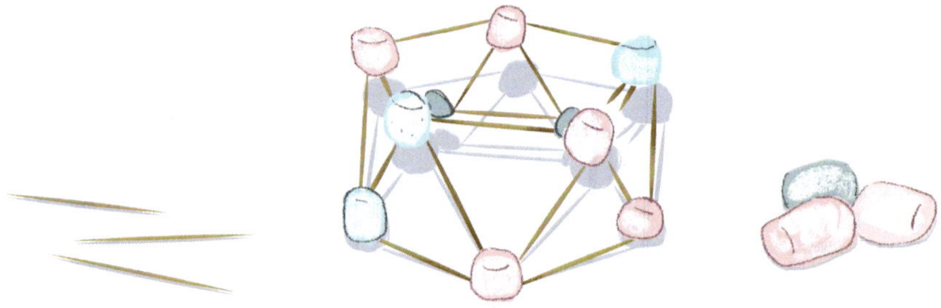